THE 14 FOREST MICE

and the

SPRING MEADOW PICNIC

By Kazuo Iwamura

English text by MaryLee Knowlton

Gareth Stevens Children's Books

MILWAUKEE

The hollow tree where the Woodmouse family
lived bustled with excitement. Papa had

decided that today was warm enough for the
first picnic of spring in Dandelion Field.

The whole family had been up since dawn.
Mama and Grandma had cooked sweet rice
dumplings and filled flasks with lemonade.
4

Petunia helped Papa and Grandpa wrap the dumplings in soft leaves.

Carrying backpacks and baskets filled with good things to eat, the Woodmice set off through the forest.

High up in the trees, a mother bird fed her new babies, while the father bird scolded the mice below.

The unfolding ferns were a sure sign of spring.
Walnut piped a merry tune on his flute for the

Woodmice on parade as the rays of the warm
sun dappled their way.

The forest was filled with the fragrance of the early spring flowers. Iris found wood violets, tiny and sweet scented.

10

The boys were too busy with their game of hide-and-seek to look at the flowers.

Then, quite suddenly, the trees ended. Ahead
of them stretched the high meadow, covered
by the bright, blue sky.

12

Chestnut climbed a tree to see if he could see Dandelion Field, but the high meadow seemed to stretch out forever.

"Let's hurry!" cried the little mice as they
bounced like springs over the soft carpet of

meadow flowers. "Watch where you land!"
called Papa. "There are nests underfoot."

A fat old toad blinked slowly as the Woodmice passed by. "He seems very large," worried

16

some of the little ones. A butterfly fluttered
to rest on Petunia's ear.

"What's that?" Peanut tugged at Grandpa.
Swirling like snakes, toad eggs floated in

the brook. The braver mice tiptoed closer
to see, but the others kept their distance.

Snails glanced up from their leafy lunch at the
parade of Woodmice. "When will it be time

for our lunch?" asked Peanut. "Soon, soon,"
chuckled Grandpa.

At the brook, a log served as a bridge for the forest animals. But the frogs didn't need a bridge — they just jumped over the brook.

22

Hickory and Pecan jumped, too. "Be careful," begged Daisy from the bridge, as Chestnut made his daring leap.

Oops! Kersplash! Hickory pulled a dripping
Cashew out of the water as their brothers

laughed merrily. "Everyone falls in the first time they jump," soothed Hickory.

The parade continued. Then, suddenly, Daisy cried "Look!" The tiny white parachutes

floating on the breeze told the Woodmice
they were nearing Dandelion Field.

Picnic time at long last! The rice dumplings were delicious. And for dessert, a surprise of

sweet wrinkled raisins, all washed down with
tart lemonade.

Watched by their meadow friends, they joined hands for a circle game. What a gay finish to their best spring picnic ever!

30

The Woodmouse family was happy as they headed for home. They knew that this picnic was just the beginning . . .

For a free color catalog describing Gareth Stevens' list of high-quality books, call
1-800-542-2595 (USA) or 1-800-461-9120 (Canada). Gareth Stevens' Fax: (414) 225-0377.

THE 14 FOREST MICE
THE 14 FOREST MICE and the SPRING MEADOW PICNIC
THE 14 FOREST MICE and the SUMMER LAUNDRY DAY
THE 14 FOREST MICE and the HARVEST MOON WATCH
THE 14 FOREST MICE and the WINTER SLEDDING DAY

Library of Congress Cataloging-in-Publication Data

Iwamura, Kazuo, 1939-
The fourteen forest mice and the spring meadow picnic / by Kazuo Iwamura ;
[English text, MaryLee Knowlton]. — North American ed.
p. cm. — (The Fourteen forest mice)
Summary: Members of the Forest Mouse family enjoy the delights of nature
as they go on an invigorating spring picnic.
ISBN 0-8368-0498-8 (lib.bdg.)
ISBN 0-8368-1146-1 (trade)
[1. Mice—Fiction. 2. Picnicking—Fiction. 3. Nature—Fiction.] I. Knowlton, MaryLee, 1946- .
II. Title. III. Title: 14 forest mice and the spring meadow picnic.
IV. Series: Iwamura, Kazuo, 1939- Fourteen forest mice.
PZ7.I954Foc 1991   [E]—dc20   90-50704

North American edition first published in 1991 by
Gareth Stevens Publishing
1555 North RiverCenter Drive, Suite 201
Milwaukee, Wisconsin 53212, USA

This U.S. edition copyright © 1991. Text copyright © 1991 by Gareth Stevens, Inc.
First published in Japan as *Juyonhiki No Pikunikku* (Fourteen mice go on a picnic) by
Kazuo Iwamura. Original book design by Takahisa Kamijo. Copyright © 1986 by
Kazuo Iwamura. English translation rights arranged with Doshin-sha through
Japan Foreign-Rights Centre.

Design: Kristi Ludwig

Printed in the United States of America

2 3 4 5 6 7 8 9 99 98 97 96 95 94